PZ
7
.B452225
S65
2005

P9-DMB-823

170301

SNIP SNAP!

What's That?

RECEIVED MAY 12

By Mara Bergman *Illustrated by* Nick Maland

RECEIVED
MAY - 2006
SENECA LIBRARIES
KING CAMPUS

Greenwillow Books *An Imprint of* HarperCollins*Publishers*

Snip Snap! What's That?
Text copyright © 2005 by Mara Bergman. Illustrations copyright © 2005 by Nick Maland.
First published in 2005 in Great Britain by Hodder Children's Books. First published in 2005 in the United States by Greenwillow Books, an imprint of HarperCollins Publishers. The right of Mara Bergman to be identified as the author and Nick Maland as the illustrator of this work has been asserted by them. All rights reserved. Manufactured in China. www.harperchildrens.com

The full-color art was prepared with watercolor on photocopied drawings.
The text type is 22-point Latienne.

Library of Congress Cataloging-in-Publication Data

Bergman, Mara.
Snip snap!: what's that? / by Mara Bergman ; pictures by Nick Maland.
p. cm.
"Greenwillow Books."
Summary: Three siblings are frightened by the wide mouth, long teeth, and strong jaws of the alligator who has crept up the stairs—until they decide they have had enough.
ISBN 0-06-077754-0 (trade).
[1. Alligators—Fiction. 2. Fear—Fiction. 3. Brothers and sisters—Fiction.]
I. Maland, Nick, ill. II. Title.
PZ7.B452225Sn 2005 [E]—dc22 2004013420

First American Edition 10 9 8 7 6 5 4 3 2 1

Greenwillow Books

For Marissa, Eva,
and Jonathan, with love
—M. B.

For Mum and Dad
—N. M.

When the alligator
came *creeping* . . .
creeping . . .

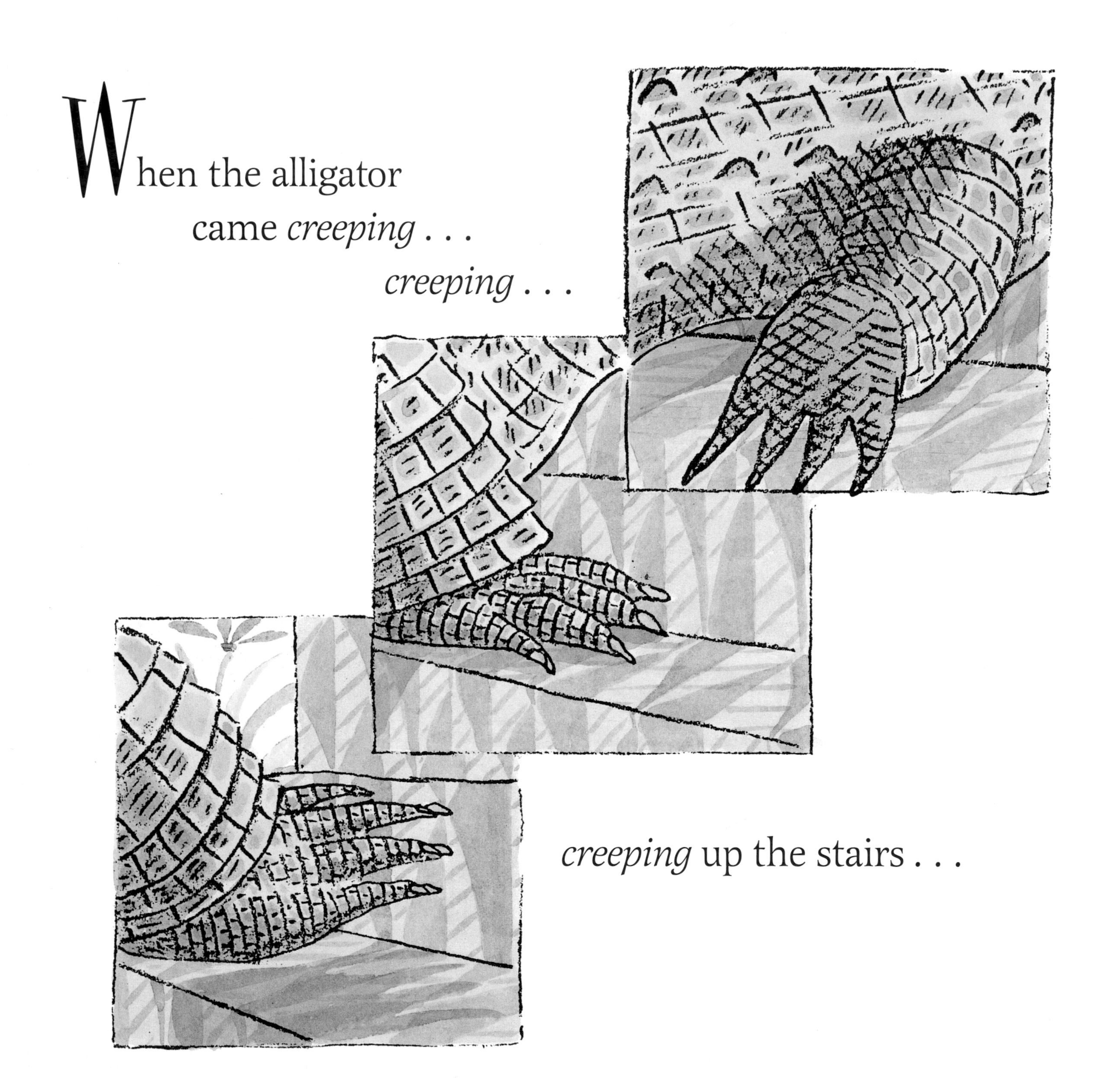

creeping up the stairs . . .

13
were the children scared?

YOU BET THEY WERE!

Marissa tried to close the door.
Eva tried and tried some more.
And Jonathan didn't try at all,
he just cried
and cried
and cried . . .

then he hid.

The alligator's mouth was wide.
Its teeth were long.
Its jaws were strong.
The children watched as it began
to bite the edges of the door.

Were the children scared?

YOU BET THEY WERE!

The alligator
slithered . . .
slithered . . .
slithered . . .
down the hall,

and slipped into the living room.

It *swishhhhhhed* and *swooooooshed* its tremendous tail,

which was shiny and spiked
and full of scales.

Were the children scared?

YOU BET THEY WERE!

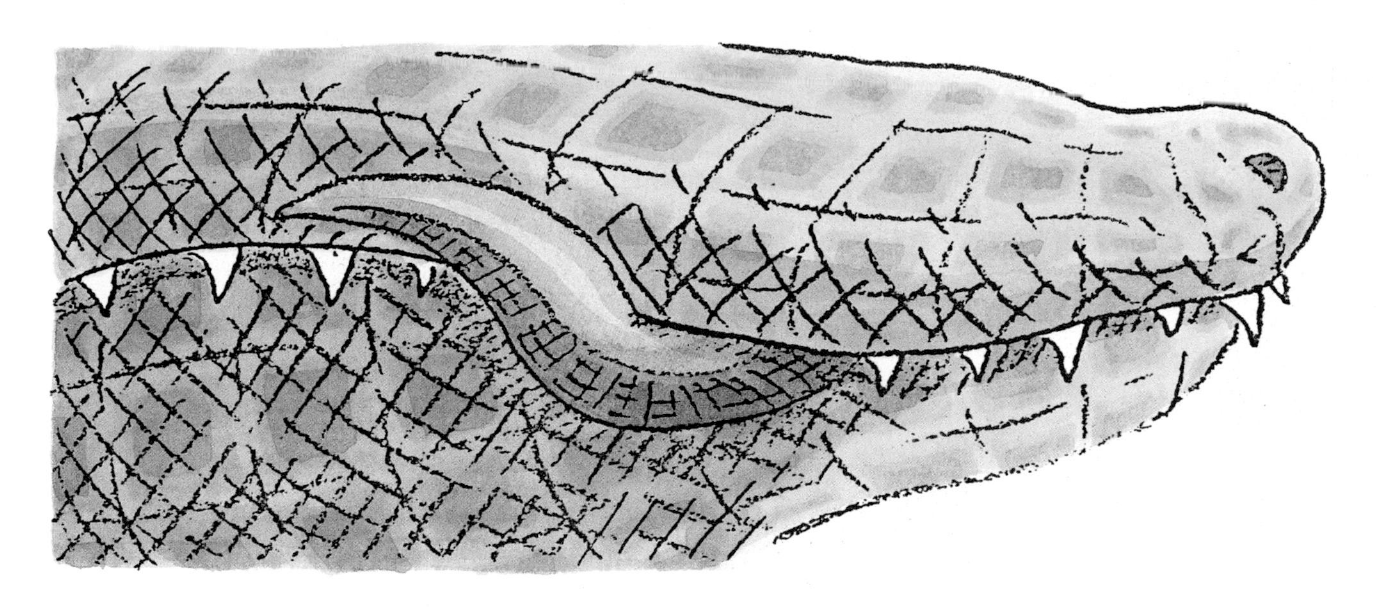

The alligator's tongue was flicking.

The alligator's feet were kicking.

Then the alligator's mouth
opened up v-e-r-y wide,
creak . . . creak . . . creak . . . ,

as if to invite the children inside.

Were the children scared?

YOU BET THEY WERE!

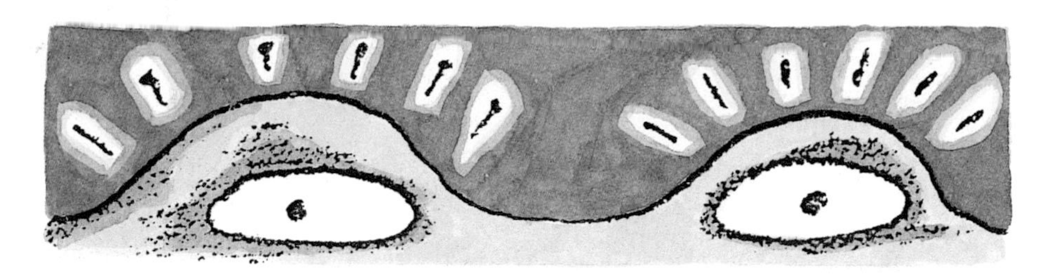

The alligator’s eyes were flashing.

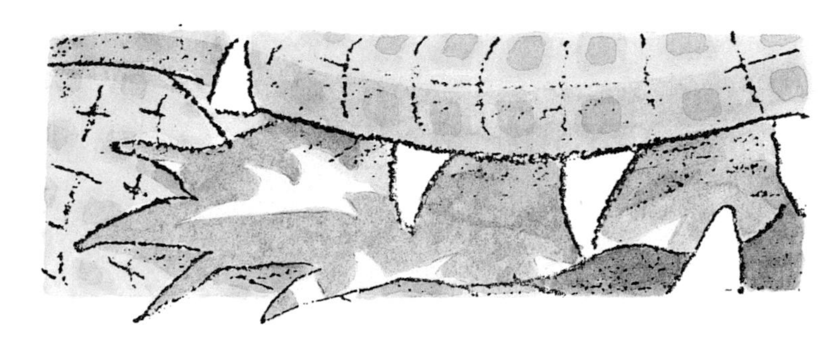

The alligator’s teeth were gnashing,
as tables and chairs and the piano went crashing.

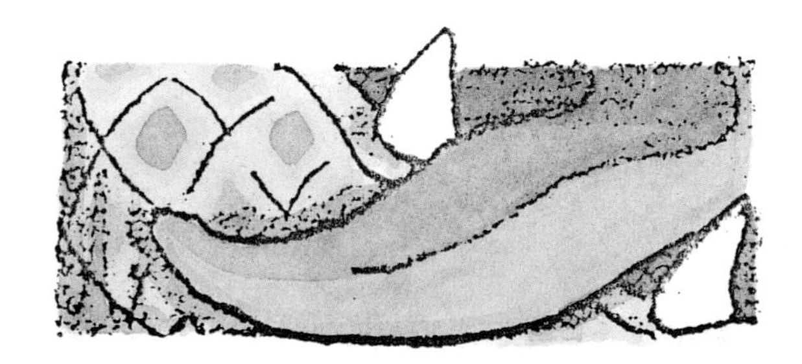

And after the sofa and curtains were ripped,
the alligator licked its lips.

Were the children scared?

YOU BET THEY WERE!

And then what did the alligator do?
Did it say to the children,
"I'm going to eat you?"

Well, not exactly, but . . .

it came closer . . .

and closer . . .

and closer until . . .

The children decided they'd had enough
of all this scary alligator stuff.

They plucked up their courage,
and gave a great shout:

"ALLIGATOR,
YOU GET OUT!"
And was the alligator scared?

YOU
BET
IT
WAS!

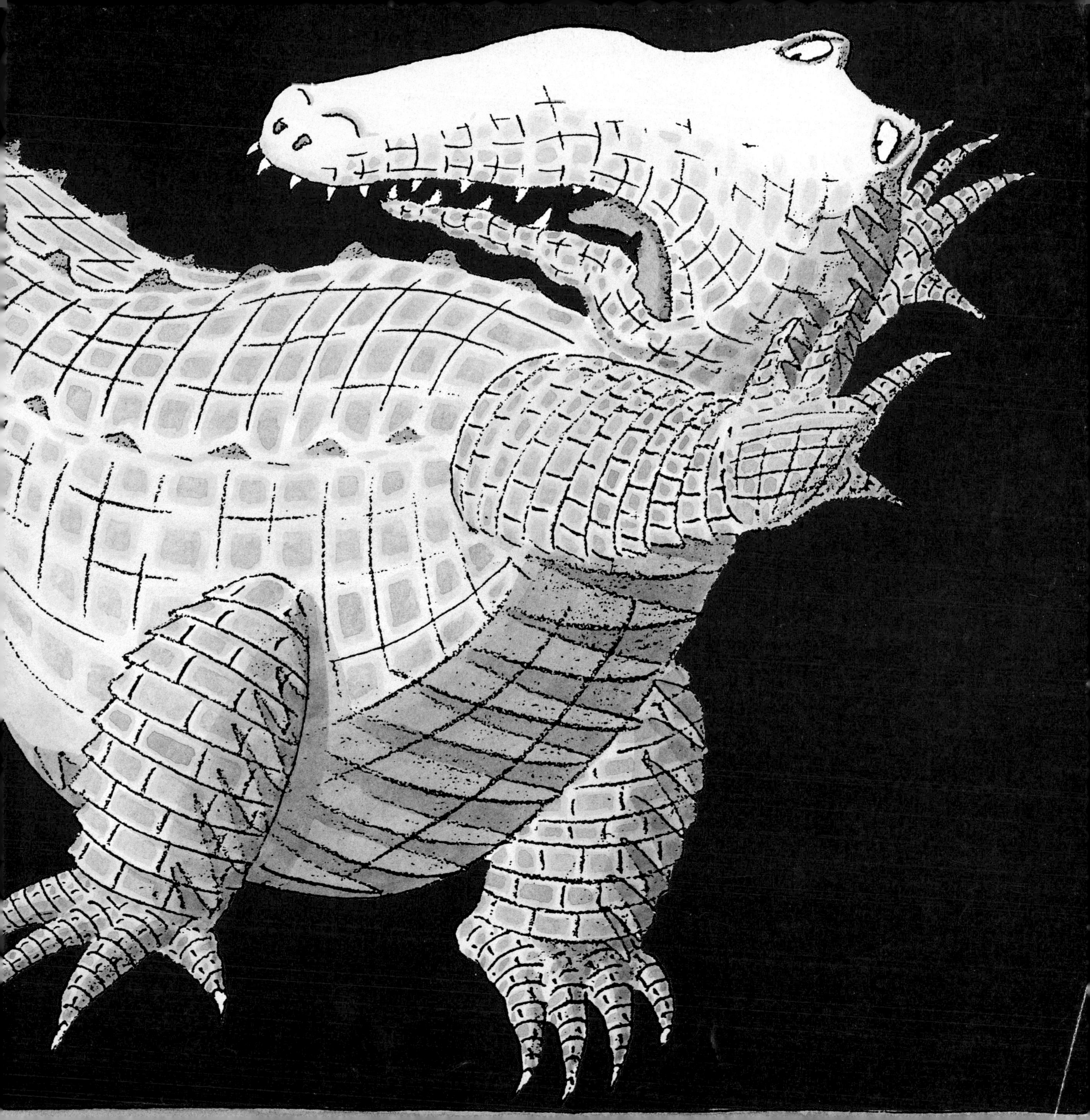

Thump
bump
bump
thump!

And the alligator went stumbling, tumbling, grumbling . . .
Swoooooooooooooooooooooooosssssssssssssssshhhhhhhhhhhhhhhh . . .

all the way home!

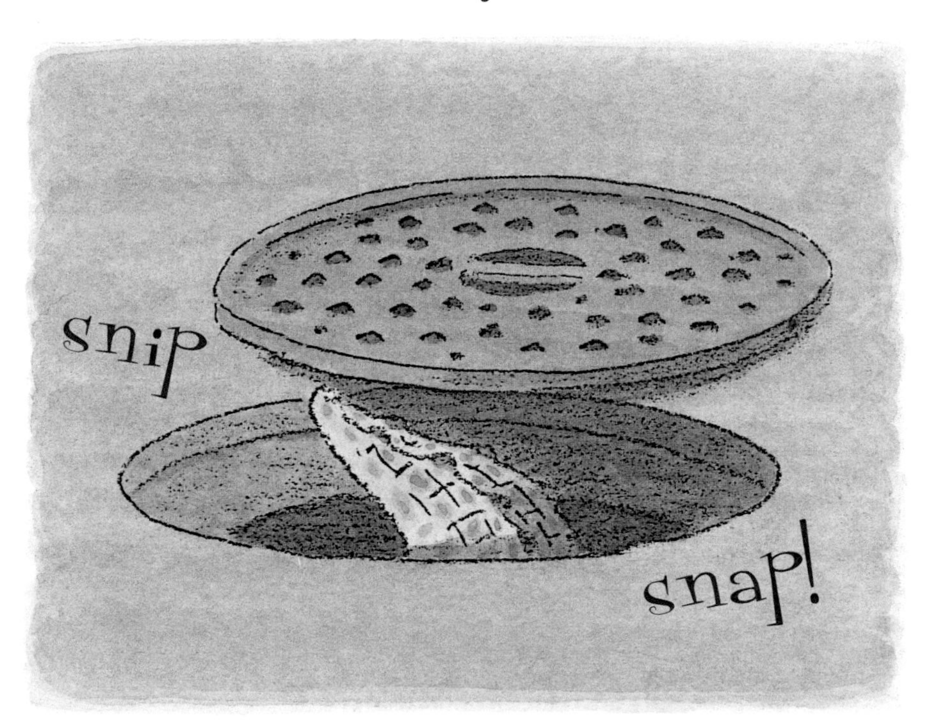

The End.